Table Of Contents

There's Something About

Table Seven

Stories
by
Theresa Snyder
Brian K. Larson
James W. McAllister

Book Concept, Format, Cover Design
and Artwork
by
Theresa Snyder, Brian K. Larson, and
James W. McAllister

To friends, near and far

There's Something About Table Seven

James W. McAllister

The pretty blonde stopped at the door. Her left hand lifted her purse as her right brushed away the snow and opened it.

"Where is that key…"

"Look under the kitchen sink you carry in that thing!" The short, dark man patted the side of her purse.

"Oh, Fred. Very funny. Ha. Ha."

"I've got my key. Really, Donna, you should just knock. Joel will let you in."

"He's so busy in the kitchen, he gets upset if I pull him away from prep."

Fred unlocked the door and held it open, "After you, my dear."

"Always the gentleman, Mr. Malcom."

"Always the lady, Miss Evergreen," Fred bowed extravagantly as she walked past.

"Good afternoon Joel," Ellie called.

"Heya, Jo!" Fred echoed.

The clang of pots and pans hitting the floor drowned out the rumble of Joel's reply.

Fred hung his coat and held his hand out for Donna's. He hung her coat next to his and slipped into the kitchen. Donna tied her apron as she walked to the greeter's station. She flicked the podium's light on.

"Another full house up to ten. And Jack didn't assign tables. Again. Must be more than one 'special occasion'."

Fred backed into the dining area with a tub of glasses balanced on top of a tub of napkin-wrapped silverware.

"Here you go, luv. You set the tables and I'll assign 'em to the reservations."

The door's bell tinkled.

"Must be…"

"Ellie."

"'Ello, all," an almost-faded Cockney accent sang through a mischievous smile.

"Yep. Afternoon, Ellie."

"'Ow's it lookin' t'night, Fred?"

"Full 'til ten. Looks like a string of 'specials'."

"Can I 'ave tables five ta eight then? I 'ad one ta fout the last two nights…"

"That's fine with me Fred."

"All set then. Donna, set up the silverware, Ellie can do the glasses. I'll get the specials' menu from Joel. The new waitress starts today. Jack should be…"

The door tinkled at Fred's cue.

"Afternoon, afternoon." a bartender's grin carried a thin dark moustache into the restaurant. Jack hung his hat and coat, then pulled his apron from the rack.

He effortlessly tied it behind his waist and lifted the bar gate.

"What's new, Jack!" Fred waved.

"New York, New Jers…"

"Very funny. These reservations," Fred pointed to the paper on the podium, "You left the tables open…"

"Again!" Donna added.

2

"Did not," Jack walked up behind Fred and peered over his shoulder.

"Did so!" Fred tapped the paper.

"There's only one reservation on the books… For Table Seven…"

"It's him, isn't it."

"Well I'll be…"

"You sure you assigned 'em all?" Fred whispered.

"Absolutely."

"Donna, better …"

"You know what will happen."

"Again?"

Once more the door's bell tinkled. Anxious eyes poked in and looked around.

"Well come on in girl, we can't afford to heat the outdoors!"

The girl looked too young. Silver and green eyes, bright red cheeks, and glowing nose entered under a brown knit cap.

"You must be Cindy."

"Yes, I, uh, ummm…"

"Don't be shy child! Flash that smile if ya wan' good tips! Better than flashing yer…"

"Ellie!"

"Fred, you gonna give her…"

"Of course he isn't," Donna took the girl's coat and hung it on the rack. "Not on her first night."

"Welcome aboard, Cindy. I'm Fred, this is Ellie, Donna, and Jack's behind the bar. Tony is…" Fred looked around the empty restaurant, "Late. You can take tables nine and ten tonight. Donna, you take eleven and twelve too."

Donna stuck her tongue out at Fred.

"I saw that. Where is Tony?"

"Audition, I bet," Donna shrugged.

"Regular Frank Sinatra," Fred mumbled.

"Come 'ere, dearie. I'll show ya the ropes." Ellie leaned closer to the girl's head and whispered, "Be careful of Freddie. 'E's got eyes in the back of 'is 'ead, 'e does!"

"I heard that. Ellie, you help Cindy with nine, Donna can back up on ten."

"Hello, Cindy!" Jack set his elbow on the bar, leaned forward, and rested his square chin in his hand. His dark eyes flashed brightly, "Do you know, Cindy is one of my top-ten favorite female names?"

"Knock it off, Jack." Ellie bent her head in Jack's direction, "He's harmless unless you get to know him," Donna led the girl to the pick-up station. "This is where you put the orders. Here is where the food comes out."

Cindy's head was turning right and left.

"'Ave ya ever waitressed before, dearie?" Ellie asked.

Cindy nodded her head.

"Can you speak?" Donna put her hand on Cindy's shoulder.

"Yes. I'm just a little… nervous, I guess."

"You'll be fine. Here, here's the order tab. Just write the table and seat number here, then check what they order. Stick the order slip here…"

"Okay, ladies!" Joel's tenor chimed from the kitchen, kitchen, followed by the appearance of a chubby, grey-haired man in chef's whites. "Oh, hello Cindy. I see you've met everyone. Good. Here are tonight's specials!"

—

Just what the Doctor Ordered

James W. McAllister

"I can't believe it." Doctor Smith whispered as he stepped back from the bedside.

Four in one week.

"I don't think we can do any more. She's gone. Does everyone agree?"

"Yes, Doctor," was repeated by each of the nurses and respiratory therapists in the room.

"Time of death… three PM." He picked up the chart and scribbled a signature. "I'll dictate a note later," Dr. Smith mumbled and walked out of the room, almost running into the Chief Medical Officer.

"Charlie, come with me."

"Ralph, I'm not in the mood."

"Get in the mood. We need to talk now," Doctor Ralph Hornsby turned and headed for his office without waiting for a reply.

Dr. Smith followed.

Charlie had seen the dark-stained woodwork and book lined walls of Ralph Hornsby's office many times before. He'd been a frequent visitor, arguing, pleading, begging, for funding for more staff, for an ICU improvement, or for a new ventilator. As the hospital's head trauma surgeon he saw improving the hospital as his job.

"Have a seat, Charlie. Rough code."

"Yeah. They all are."

"You ran it well. Even you can't fix a shredded ventricle. Something else is bothering you, I saw it, I still see it in your eyes. What is it?"

"Four. Four dead in six days. Ralph, I'm not good enough."

"Bull. You're the best trauma surgeon on the East Coast. If we were in your office I'd show you the certifications, honors, and awards to prove it..."

"I couldn't save them, Ralph. I..." Charlie's voice darkened, "I don't know if I can keep doing this."

Ralph frowned and drummed his fingers lightly on his desk.

"Feeling burned out?"

"Feeling worthless."

"All physicians go through that from time to time. It's why we invented vacations."

"A vacation won't help."

"Hmm... Tell you what..." Ralph hit his intercom, "Sheila, make a reservation for one at Hunter's Bar and Grill. Ask for Table Seven." Ralph sat back and looked over the rims of his bifocals, "Get cleaned up. You have about 45 minutes. It's three blocks west."

Charlie walked slowly up to the wooden door, wondering if the place was open.

Why would Ralph think this would help? I'm just not good enough anymore, worn out, washed up, burned out. I need to go sell houses or something.

The door opened to his push.

"Welcome! You must be..." Fred glanced at the reservation list, "Doctor Smith! Your table is ready sir, right this way."

Charlie followed Fred to the indicated table.

I'd better stay clear of the red wine. I couldn't handle seeing a red stain on white linen.

Charlie sat in the far chair.

"Your server will be Ellie tonight, Dr. Smith. She'll be right along."

"Thanks," Charlie looked around the room, taking in the brilliant white tablecloths seeming to float above the hardwood floor. Fred led people to the surrounding tables every few seconds it seemed.

The place is filling up fast. Must be good food then.

A movement caught his attention.

"'Ello, love. I'm Ellie. May I offer you a beverage?"

"Just water please."

"Right away Dr. Smith."

The moment Ellie left, Cindy walked up to table seven.

"Excuse me, Doctor Smith. I wanted to thank you for trying to save my father. It was three years ago he was car jacked and run over. John Kincaid was his name."

"Kincaid.. He, he didn't... I'm so sorry. Please forgi..."

"No! You worked so hard. I could see you through the glass in the Emergency Room. I just wanted, no, that's not right. I had to say thank you for trying so hard!"

Charlie stared at the young waitress. As she walked away, Fred led a woman and a young girl past Charlie's table.

"Excuse me, I must stop," the woman tugged at Fred's sleeve. "Sir, aren't you Dr. Smith from Memorial?"

"Yes, I am. If I…"

"Doctor! I can't thank you enough! Here, my daughter Julie, you…" she wiped a tear, "you saved her last year. She was in that awful train wreck. She had…"

"Oh, mother! You're intruding. Let the Doctor eat!"

"She had a dozen chest tubes in her. Everyone said she had no chance, but you wouldn't hear it. You pulled her through…" She took a big breath, "Well, anyway, thank you Doctor! Enjoy your meal, and God bless you!"

"Thanks…"

She was that little girl, pinned under the wreckage when the subway car derailed. Crushed chest. She was too badly injured to live and too young to die.

"'Ere you are Doctor. Have you decided yet?"

"Thank you, eh, Ellie. I'll have the… em… Clams. I'll have the clams in garlic and white wine please. And a glass of Chardonnay."

"Coming right up Doctor!" Ellie swirled off as the Doctor watched Fred lead an older couple to a nearby table. He watched them sit down, the man glancing at him several times before Ellie set his wine down. He noticed Cindy, the young waitress who had thanked him, waiting on their table.

"Your dinner will be out shortly Doctor Smith."

"Thank you Ellie," Charlie stared into the glass, swirled it a little, and sipped the wine.

White tablecloths. White napkins, like an ER Trauma Room... No, every other table has red napkins. I wonder why mine are white? He noticed the older couple talking to a young waitress. Something moved in Charlie's peripheral vision.

"Em, eh…" A voice came from a middle age man in a neck brace standing slightly behind Charlie, "Excuse me, but you are Doctor Charles Smith, aren't you?"

"Yes. Do I know you, sir?"

"I don't think so. We have met though, I'm told. Three months ago, a car cut me off and.... They told me it was you. They said you did it…" The man gulped and reached his hand out towards the Doctor, "You pulled me out of the burning car, and stayed with me until the ambulance arrived. I, I'm sorry I didn't contact you sooner, but, well…" he raised his hand a little, "Thank you. You likely saved my life!"

"It wasn't anything anyone wouldn't have done," Charlie shook the man's hand.

"Not true. They told me my car had been there for at least ten minutes before you stopped to help. A lot of cars go by that spot in ten minutes. Only you stopped. A few minutes after you pulled me out my car burst into flames. You saved my life."

"Well, I…"

"I don't want to intrude. Enjoy your meal. And, thank you again!"

I never thought a thing about that. His car was burning. I just pulled him out and called 911.

"Your dinner, sir!" Ellie set the plate down, "Would you like some freshly grated Parmesan?"

"No, thank you Ellie."

"Well, you enjoy your dinner, Doctor Smith!"

Charlie twirled his fork in the pasta and stabbed a clam. He'd just lifted his fork ever so slightly when…

"Excuse me, but are you…"

"Doctor Charles Smith," he set his fork down. "May I help you, miss?"

"Doctor, my cousin, he came home today."

"Good news, I guess…"

"Oh, forgive me. My cousin is William Steele. You were the trauma surgeon, you stopped his bleeding and saved his kidney. He was in the hospital for six months. I looked up the chances for the surgery you did, one time in a dozen it works. You saved his life, Doctor. I just wanted to say 'Thank you'. Please, I've interrupted your dinner. Thank you Doctor!" The young woman bent quickly and planted a light kiss on his forehead before she vanished.

Dr. Smith savored a clam as Ellie walked up.

"How is everything, Dr. Smith?"

"Mmm…" He swallowed quickly, "Fine Ellie. Thank you."

"Glad to hear it," she smiled and headed for the kitchen.

A smartly dressed man walked boldly up to the Doctor's table, "Excuse me, but are you the trauma surgeon, Dr. Smith?"

"Yes, I am. May I help you?"

"You already have, doctor. Me, and a lot of other people. You see, the owner of the company I work for was a patient of yours. He dove off of a boat last year and ended up with a broken neck. You patched him up, gave him the ability to come back and run the business again. With him out, we couldn't get any new contracts. The company would have closed its doors if he didn't come back when he did. He just signed two new contracts that saved the company, saved all of our jobs. Doctor, you saved his life, and you saved 87 jobs too. Thank you sir," the man turned and walked back to his table before Charlie could say anything.

Ralph must have set this up. All this can't be a coincidence...

"Charlie! Excuse me, dear, I'll be along in a moment," The tall man held out his hand as Fred led the pretty woman to another table.

"Stan, Hi," Charlie half stood as he shook his hand. "Did Ralph send you too?"

"Ralph? No, Gina and I have had this reservation for months. This is a hard place to get into. Why would you think Ralph had..."

"People keep coming up to me, thanking me for..."

"Oh, I see," Stan looked around a little, then glanced at the table cloth. "Charlie, have you been, well, stressed out lately?"

"Yeah, Quite a bit."

"Trauma surgery. Don't know how you do it. Hip and knee replacements get to me after a while, don't know how you handle the trauma," A thin smile flashed as Stan sat in the empty chair.

"You see, *this* place," he tapped the table, "can be…"

"Excuse me, sir," a man with greying hair stopped next to the table, "Aren't you Doctor Stanley Munson, the orthopedic surgeon?"

"Yes, I am."

"I thought so. You replaced my hips last year. Thank you, the pain is gone, and I'm good as new!" He held his hand out and Stan shook it. "Well, I won't interrupt your dinner. Thank you, Doctor!"

"You're welcome, sir!" Stan replied as the man walked away.

"Charlie," Stan stood up, "When did Ralph send you here?"

"This afternoon…" he stared at the man walking away, "about 3:45."

"And you think he got reservations for all these former patients in what, fifteen minutes?" Stan stood up, "Charlie, enjoy it. You deserve what happens tonight. Now, I've got a wife to pamper."

Charlie managed to eat half of his dinner, despite three more interruptions. When the remaining clams and pasta hit room temperature he motioned to Ellie to clear his plate.

"Will the Good Doctor be 'aving desert tonight?"

"No thank you, Ellie. It's been wonderful. I'll have the check please."

"Oh, there's no check, sir. The couple that sat there," she motioned to a nearby table, the one with the older couple, the man who kept looking at him had sat, "Cindy waited on them tonight. They come in twice a week, you know. Well, they paid your check, Doctor. And they gave Cindy this note for you," Ellie set the folded paper on the table. "Enjoy the rest of the evening, Doctor!"

"You too, Ellie." Charlie unfolded and began to read.

Dear Doctor Smith. You don't know us, but you do know our daughter. She interned with you last year. We wanted to thank you for the inspiration you gave her. She was ready to drop out before she met you. She says you inspired her, gave her direction. This week she has accepted a position with Community Hospital as their trauma surgeon.

Thank you Doctor.

Charlie pulled out his cell phone and hit a speed dial number as he walked out. As the Hunter's Bar and Grille's door closed behind him, he said, "Yeah. Ralph, thank you. The dinner? I honestly don't remember. It was the most amazing evening though…"

Every Journey Ends With A Single Step

James W. McAllister

He paused, just a moment. Up, down, around. His eyes drank the familiar sights this last time.

The brownish red color of the wooden door. The pattern of the grain. The stains from decades of rain on the concrete steps.

The dark gold tones of the oxidized brass.

"I need to remember this place. I've always been comfortable here. Oh, well, what is the old saying? Every journey ends with a single step…"

He pulled the grey fedora from his head and reached for the door.

The brass handle chilled his palm.

"Mr. Hayes! So nice to see you again!" Fred called.

"Good evening Fred. Nice to be in town again."

"Your table will be a few minutes. Please have a seat at the bar, the first drink is on Joe!"

"Thanks, Fred." Harold Hayes walked slowly to the bar, "Joe! How are you?"

"Mr. Hayes! I've got a seat right here for you, front and center. Glenfiddich neat? The first one's on Fred."

Harold smiled at the familiar banter as he set his fedora and coat on the hat tree. He pulled the barstool out, and swung a leg into the lady next to him. "Excuse me, Miss, but I've never quite mastered the art of climbing onto a barstool."

"Oh, don't worry about it." Something about her looked familiar. "You seem to be a regular here?"

"Yes, I make it a point to eat here at least once whenever I'm in town. Harold's the name. Do you come here much, Miss?" She looked a lot like…

"No, no. I've never been here before. Call me Helen. I'm just here because… Oh, it's silly, really."

"Here ya go, Mr. Hayes," Joe set the golden Scotch on the bar.

Helen's head tilted at Joe's words.

"Special occasion?"

"Well, my mother passed away recently," she looked to her wine, "Her will said I had to have dinner here to collect my inheritance. There isn't much, really, just a small insurance policy. I wasn't going to bother, but tonight's the last night before it all goes to charity, and I thought, well, why not?"

"I'm sorry to hear about your mom."

"Oh, thank you. She passed three weeks ago. Chronic health problems brought on by living a fast life. The thing is, I have to have dinner tonight, and they're booked solid. I only get a table if someone doesn't show up."

"Well, if you don't mind sharing a table with a man old enough to be your father, you may dine with me, if that's not too forward."

"Why, thank you! That's kind of you," Helen shot a glance at the man's left hand. The faintest hint of a smile reflected off of the gold band there.

"Mr. Hayes!" A faded brogue echoed delightfully through the bar. "So wonderful to see ya ag'in, Sir!"

"Ellie," Harold smiled, "as lovely and kind as always!"

"Yer table's ready, right this way. Would ya like another Scotch at the table, or a nice red wine?"

"A red would be wonderful, Ellie. This young lady will be joining me tonight," Harold offered his hand to invite Helen.

Helen shot an inquiring look to the waitress as she set one foot on the floor.

"Oh, Missy, Mr. Hayes is a perfect gentleman. You'll have a grand time." Ellie glanced at the empty wine glass in front of Helen, "Another red wine for you too, Miss?"

Helen smiled and took the older man's hand, "Thank you. Ellie, isn't it?"

"Right this way now, Table Seven's all set for two."

Ellie soon had the two seated and the drinks served.

"So, Mr... Hayes, is it? What brings you to town?"

"I work in healthcare accreditation. I travel all over the country, but since I live near the coast, I'm often assigned here. This place is like a home away from home to me. But, it's a bittersweet trip this time."

"Oh? Why is that?"

"This is my last trip here. I'm retiring. Friday is my last survey."

"Well, that's not sad. You and your wife will be..."

"Oh, I'm not married. Not anymore. Not for…" he sighed, "not for a long time…" Harold's left thumb rubbed the gold ring on his left hand. He stared at the reflected lights in his wine and sighed. "Anyway, I'm selling my place upstate and moving south. No one there since my brother passed last year, so nothing to hold me. I do have…" Harold swallowed and sighed again. "So, tell me, if it's not too nosey of me to ask, what are your plans? You said something about moving?"

"I don't know. There's nothing to keep me in the city. I just stayed for mom, not that it really meant anything to her. That's not fair, she didn't know these last few years. She was sort of, well, a hippie. Free and easy, never met a responsibility she couldn't shirk. When I was about twenty, her mind started to go. By the time I was twenty five, I was taking care of her. I figure after twenty years of caring for her, I should figure out what *I* want to do now."

"That's rough. Dementia can bring a lot of stress to a family."

"Oh, there is no family. Just me now. I never knew my dad, mom never would talk about him. The last two years she'd call out a name, but nothing else. Since we're being so personal, how did you lose your wi…"

Harold's eyes frantically searched. He smiled at Ellie standing next to the table.

"Excuse me folks, but are you two ready to order?"

"Shrimp cocktail and the filet with peppercorn-mushroom demi-glace, please Ellie. Helen?"

"Sounds nice. Ellie, separate checks, please?"

"No problem, sweetie. How would you like your steak, Miss Helen?"

"Medium, please."

"And Mr. Hayes, just a tad past medium-rare, as usual?"

"You're the best, Ellie."

"So, since you keep changing the subject, and for some strange reason I feel I can trust you, I'll be blunt. What happened to your wife?"

"Well," he swallowed hard, "she left. One day we were happy, expecting our first born, the next day she was gone. Three weeks later I get divorce papers in the mail, and a restraining order forbidding me from seeing her. I never had a clue she wasn't happy. I never hurt her, never touched her in anger, I never even yelled at her…"

Harold swallowed a large nothing.

"I'm sorry. I didn't mean to bring up your pain."

"That's OK. I never talk about it, so it's probably good to get it out."

"You still wear the ring."

"Couldn't bear to take it off. The last fifteen years I can't take it off! Ha-ha."

"Do you have a picture of your wife?"

"Do you have a picture of your mom?"

Wallet.

Purse.

Pictures held out.

Harold moved sideways in his seat.

Helen's hand went to her throat.

"She looks just like…"

"It can't be!"

"What was your wife's name?"

"What was your mom's name?"

"Oh!"

"Well… So, what do we…"

"We take it one step at a time," Helen smiled through tears,

"Dad!"

The Big Question

Theresa Snyder

Megan tried for the third time to fasten the clasp on her necklace. Once again, it slipped from her shaking hands.

"The Hell with it," she huffed and laid it back down on the dresser. She'd just go without it.

The dress she chose to wear for her evening with John was one of her favorites for the holiday season, but tonight it felt tight in the waist. After adjusting her swollen breasts, she eventually added a pin to pull the neckline together and show some modesty.

She had to tell him tonight. She frowned. What a great holiday present to lay on a guy. *'Oh, by the way John, I'm nine weeks pregnant.'* She cringed at the thought.

Why? Why, had she fucked up her life in such a royal way? She was headed toward one of the top positions in the publishing firm she worked for. She would make senior editor by next summer. As much as she wanted a baby, she didn't need one right now.

It was the damned teddy bear's fault. She could see it in the reflection of the mirror on its shelf with the rest of the collection behind her. Yeah, the teddy, and raging hormones that told her she was getting past the years of conception and might miss out on that bundle of joy. She ran her hand over her very slight 'baby bump.'

John Lakey had totally won her over. He was smooth online and dashing on their first date. He had done his homework, Googled her, and found out she collected 'tiny teddies.' He arrived with one in hand when he picked her up. It was all dressed up in a British soldier's uniform and had its arms wrapped around a magnum of champagne. She should have known better. She could always hold her hard liquor, but champagne went straight to her... it made her feel 'Sexy as Hell.'

Their meal that first night must have been expensive, and it seemed right to ask him in for a nightcap. He was attractive, had a good job. And he made her laugh. What was the harm? Megan ran her hand over her belly again. "It wouldn't be right to call you 'harm,' would it." Luckily, the full skirt of her dress would hide it.

Too many scenarios were running through her head. If he was not overjoyed to hear she was pregnant, did she raise the child on her own or give it up for adoption? Could she give it up? "My baby..." But could she raise a child alone, and hold down a job with growing responsibility? She was so stressed she wondered why her hair hadn't fallen out. Instead, it had become this glossy mane of chestnut waves. The doctor said it was a side effect of pregnancy for some women.

What did she know about John anyway? They had only been seeing each other for a little over two months. Yes, they had spent time online getting to know each other before they even met in person, but she didn't even know if he liked kids. They hadn't gotten that far in their relationship. She chuckled to herself, "It seems we have!"

Megan looked at herself one last time in the mirror. Oh, she wished she had never met John Lakey.

"Lakey – table for two," Fred announced.

"Right this way please," Donna smiled. "Your waitress, Ellie, will be right with you."

John and Megan followed her to their table. John seated Megan and then took his own position across from her.

Donna leaned down to offer the wine list, and whispered in his ear. "Table Seven - the best seat in the house, as requested."

John smiled and thanked her.

"Ellie will be with you in just a moment," Donna nodded and went back to her station at the podium by the door.

John looked over the top of the wine list. "How about some champagne tonight to celebrate the season?"

"I'm kind of chilly. I think I'll stick with coffee for the moment," Megan said. '*Oh, and by the way, I'm pregnant and can't drink for the next year.*' She shook her head. She was going to have to stop this running internal dialogue.

"Sure… okay…" John looked a bit disappointed, but when the waitress showed up he ordered coffee for both of them.

"I didn't get a chance to tell you that my sister called and invited us for New Year's Day."

"Us?" Megan asked.

"Yeah, well, I told her a bit about you." He ran his hand through his dark hair – the gesture made Megan think of a young boy trying not to look nervous. It always made her smile. "I thought we could drive up together. It's lovely in the winter. Her place is very secluded. Jake works from home, and the kids are homeschooled, so they're all cozy in their place." John looked hopefully to Megan. Since the coffee arrived, she seemed to be more interested in her cup than him. "They have this great two story, log cabin, with all the amenities. I told you Janet is a collector, so the house is really special. Lots of antiques. I know you two will hit it off."

Megan looked up at him and smiled. She was gorgeous tonight in a red dress. Her hair was a luscious wavy chestnut mane that fell over her shoulders. She must have put some product on it that made it shine under the subdued restaurant lights. He could almost feel it between his fingers.

"What do you say?" he asked. "It's usually fun. Janet cooks a big pot of beef stew, or soup of some kind, and she spreads the table with a selection of cheeses, meats and sourdough bread. There are munchies all over the house. She calls them her 'grazing jars' – jars full of candies and cookies. With the antique toys and the grazing jars it looks like a cross between a candy store and a toy store."

"It sounds lovely," Megan said. *'Except for one little problem… I'm pregnant! How do you feel about announcing you are going to be a father on New Year's Day along with the introduction of you new girlfriend?'*

"It really is." John took a sip of his coffee. He was doing all the talking tonight, which was not the usual. He hoped Megan was feeling okay. He didn't want anything to spoil this evening. "Is everything alright? You seem kind of distant tonight."

Megan reached up and tucked her hair behind an ear. She stared into her coffee, "I'm fine."

She looked up at him and smiled. His heart skipped a beat.

"You are so lovely tonight. You're positively glowing." He prayed he was not rushing things too fast, but he was in love. He hadn't been able to imagine his life without her since the moment he laid eyes on her.

Ellie brought the salads they ordered. John dug in, but Megan was just pushing it around her plate. He began to worry. Was she going to dump him? She had been like this the last two times they met - all quiet and withdrawn. Not bubbly like the rest of their short relationship. His sister had been surprised when he announced he would be bringing a guest. Then when he confessed that he was in love and intended to ask her to marry him, Janet had almost fainted on the other end of the line. She thought he was going to be a bachelor all his life.

He had planned to pop the question tonight, but now he was beginning to second-guess himself. What did he really know about Megan? She was orphaned at an early age and raised by foster parents. She never said how that went. Maybe she was traumatized. Maybe she was afraid of commitment and that was what he had been feeling these last couple of weeks. Maybe he should wait until after they went to his sister's to propose.

Suddenly his salad wasn't appetizing anymore. He thought about all the times she spoke to him of her work. How much she delighted in helping polish an author's manuscript. Would she be willing to give that a backseat to a relationship with him? Why hadn't he thought of this stuff before? Maybe it was even her job that was getting her down now.

"How is work going?" he asked.

"Oh, the usual," she said with a sigh. "Authors that need their manuscripts trimmed, but refuse to take any advice."

"Well, like you said a while back, a manuscript is a part of them, their baby," John said with a shrug.

'Their baby.' Megan continued to play with her food. The smell of ranch dressing, her favorite, was somehow off, as if it had gone rancid. She knew the restaurant wouldn't serve something bad. It was her 'pregnancy nose.' The doctor warned her against it in the second trimester. She just hoped the steak she ordered didn't smell as bad. Between the refusal of the champagne and the uneaten salad, John was going to know something was wrong. She was going to have to tell him soon. *'Courage, girlfriend. If he walks out you have enough leeway on your visa you can pay for the meal.'*

John had to know. He couldn't wait. He saw Ellie head toward the kitchen. The restrooms were back there too. He'd make like he needed a trip to them. "Will you excuse me?" he said and rose to his feet.

He hurried toward the back of the restaurant. When Ellie came out he boldly caught her arm and pulled her into the hall by the restrooms. She gave him a puzzled look.

"Can you do me a favor and clear the salad plates and then hold our dinner for a few minutes?" he asked.

Ellie looked concerned. "Is there somethin' wrong?"

"No, not at all. It's just that I intend to propose tonight, and I can't wait until after dessert. I want to do it now," John confessed.

Ellie smiled back at him showing, off her dimples. "That is so sweet." She reached out and squeezed his arm. "I'll get the plates right now, love. Ya just wave when ya're ready for the entre. I'll keep an eye on your table." She started to leave, but then turned back. "Good luck."

John returned to his seat. The waitress came to the table and removed their salad plates. Megan took a deep breath. She couldn't wait. She had to get this over before the next course.

"I have something I have to tell you," she started.

John interrupted her. "Me first," he said. He reached into this jacket pocket and came out with a 'tiny teddy.' It was dressed in a tux, top hat and all, and it held a sparkling diamond ring between its Velcroed paws. "Megan, will you marry me?" John said and offered it to Megan. "I need to spend the rest of my life with you."

Tears welled up in Megan's widened eyes. Her heart leapt, pushing a smile onto her face.

But she did not take the teddy or the ring. "John, I love you, but…"

His heart skipped a beat. She was going to say no. *'No… no… no… don't refuse me.'* He thought.

"I have to tell you something first." She reached across the table and squeezed his hand. "I'm pregnant."

John didn't say anything. He rose to his feet and picked up the 'tiny teddy.' *'Oh God, he's just going to walk out.'* Megan wished she could sink through a crack in the floor.

But he didn't walk out. He came around to her side of the table and knelt on one knee next to her chair. "Marry me? We will raise wonderful kids, and then we will grow old together." He took the ring out of the teddy's paws and offered it.

She held out a shaking hand. "Yes," she signed.

He slipped the ring on her finger.

Ellie, the guests at the tables around the couple, and the hostess, all broke into applause.

It will be the Death of Him

Theresa Snyder

Everyone thought Henry Huntington owned "Hunter's Bar and Grill." The establishment was well known for its diverse selection of meat from the ordinary such as beef and chicken, to the exotic of alligator and ostrich, through to the very pricey pheasant-under-glass. Henry owned the restaurant on paper, but it was Benny, The Greek who really owned the place. He used it, and several other businesses, to laundry his ill-gotten gains.

Fred breathed a sigh of relief that table seven was available when The Greek walked in at 11:00 p.m. with his two guards and Sully, his accountant. He showed them to their seats, then found Donna.

"Cover the door for a few. I need to tell Henry…"

"The Greek. I saw. Ya got it, darlin'."

Fred went back to Henry's office to tell him The Greek was here, and he didn't look like he wanted dinner. There was something about the way the bodyguards stood by the front door that made his skin crawl.

"No reservation," he told Henry. "They just showed up."

Henry closed the ledger he was writing in and pushed back from his desk.

"You seated them?"

"Table Seven was open."

"Good." Henry moved out around the desk and toward the door. "It'll be okay. I'll get a bottle of his favorite wine from the cellar." He turned back toward Fred, who had followed him to the door. "Ellie has that table tonight, but she won't serve The Greek. Normal rotation would have the new girl Cindy cover, but should we spare her this? Donna could cover, just..."

Fred shook his head. "I think we're fine. She's been doing really well tonight and the customers seem to like her. She was telling me the tips were twice what she got at her last job."

"Okay, we'll leave it as is. You better get back to the front. I'll fetch the wine."

The Greek's most impenetrable poker face stared at Sully. Though this looked like a boss taking one of the essential members of his business to dinner for a meeting, his plan was that the evening would end in blood. Sully had been warned to stay away from his daughter, Clara. The Greek couldn't afford to have any of his men disobey his orders, and Sully should have known that. This was business, and his business wouldn't last if insubordination was tolerated.

What really pissed him off was that Sully was a good accountant, and a good kid, but he couldn't have him messing up Clara's life. The Greek had plans for his daughter – a good school, a marriage outside the mob. He figured Sully didn't think he'd caught on, but The Greek didn't run the tightest mob in town by being sloppy and not noticing the details. Just this afternoon one of his men reported Sully and Carla were seen together.

The Greek's phone vibrated in his pocket, just as he saw Henry come out of the kitchen with a bottle of wine. Now that was a man who knew how to show respect. Henry never gave him any trouble. The Greek pulled his phone out and looked at the screen. It was his wife, Harriet. He didn't want to talk to her right now, he had more pressing issues. He hit the 'decline' button and laid the phone on the table beside his cutlery.

"Mr. Castellanos," Henry said in greeting as he walked up, "it's a pleasure to see you tonight. I hope you still have a taste for a fine Bordeaux?

"Of course, Henry," The Greek reached up and grabbed Henry's hand with both of his and looked straight into Henry's eyes. "Why wouldn't I?"

Henry made a show of opening the bottle pouring The Greek a taste. He waited for his approval. With a nod from The Greek, Henry poured a glass for both men. He nodded a greeting at Sully.

"We have a new waitress, Mr. Castellanos. This is her first night." Henry leaned a bit closer and lowered his voice. "I'm sure you'll like her." Henry waved Cindy over. "Cindy, this is our most important customer, Mr. Benjamin Castellanos. Treat him well."

"I'll do my best," Cindy said innocently. "May I start you with some appetizers, gentlemen?"

The Greek knew the menu by heart. He looked the young waitress up and down, never breaking that poker face. She wasn't a beauty, but she was pleasant enough and looked efficient. "Calamari for me." He nodded at Sully to add his order.

"Nothing for me," the young man answered. "I'm saving room for dessert. You make the best tiramisu in the city."

Cindy smiled at the young man. He was handsome, looked intelligent and was not wearing a ring. "I'll get that order in and out to you right away."

She stopped by the adjoining table where the bodyguards were seated and picked up an order from them for the house beer-battered onion rings and colas.

Benny's phone moved slightly on the table as its vibrating announced another call from his wife. He had a moment to wonder what-the-hell was so urgent, but he couldn't bother with it right now. He hit the 'decline' button again.

Sully sat quietly and waited for his boss to start the conversation. It was unusual for The Greek to invite support staff like Sully out to dinner, and he didn't know what this meeting was about. He knew the books were in order. He had no concerns along those lines. He was afraid this might concern Benny's daughter, Carla. Sully was attracted to her on their first meeting at a gala hosted by her father. Benny made it clear there was to be no fraternizing between his staff and any of his family members, yet Sully and Carla just kept bumping into each other. It was like fate was trying to tell them something, and today had been the topper. He could only chalk it to being at the right place at the right time.

The calamari was delivered to table seven, and the onion rings and colas to table six. The bodyguards dug in as they quietly discussed their plans for after dinner activities.

"You got the tarp put in the trunk?" Max asked Duncan.

"What kind of idiot do you think I am?" He shook his head. "No, don't answer that. Of course, I got it in the trunk. Are we taking him for a ride after dinner or doing him in the alley?"

"The boss is walking us out. He wants to make sure Sully knows why he's being put down. We'll do him in the alley and you can help me wrap and load him in the trunk. I'll dump him while you get a cab and take the boss home." Max dipped another onion ring in the sauce and stuffed it into his mouth. The idea of offing Sully did not spoil his appetite.

The conversation at table seven was tame. Nothing seemed out of place to Sully. The Greek asked if he liked the calamari, about several transactions, and the tax strategies for various accounts. Sully mentioned some ideas he had on the movement of capital, and that seemed to please The Greek. The subject of Carla was not brought up. Sully certainly was not going to say anything about it.

Benjamin Castellanos could make you evaporate and no one would dare ask where you had gone – you'd be no more than a wisp of smoke over the rooftops. Sully fidgeted, trying to decide if it was better The Greek heard about the incident from his daughter rather than him. That's what Carla insisted on. He would just keep his mouth shut, eat his meal and go home. Tomorrow would be another day, hopefully a less stressful one.

Benny squinted over a forkful of steak, wondering if he could even finish the meal without ripping the little bastard's throat out. Max had seen them no more than two blocks from his house standing in an alley, Carla wrapped in Sully's arms. The Greek's blood boiled hotter each minute.

The Greek's phone vibrated yet again. Benny poked it silent with a thump of his finger.

Sully pointed toward the phone with his fork. "Sounds like someone is anxious to talk to you tonight."

"They can wait."

"Should I go to the men's room?"

"Nah. Stay right here. They can wait."

Benny picked up his glass and took a gulp of wine. He should have just had Max and Duncan take the kid out tonight. Why did he decide to go ahead and take him to dinner? Maybe he thought the kid would confess and beg for forgiveness, he always got a kick out of that. But there he sat eating his steak and not saying a word about Clara. Why did the kid have to be such a fool? His work was exemplary. The Greek would be hard pressed to find a replacement as good as Sully.

The phone rang twice more during dinner, so when it rang in the middle of dessert, Benny decided to pick up.

"Excuse me," he said to Sully and rose from his seat.

He didn't want his wife calling him while they were dealing with Sully and the time for that was coming soon. He walked back toward the end of the bar, out of hearing range from Sully.

"Harriet, what do you need? I am in the middle of an important meeting."

"Why haven't you answered your phone? I've been trying to reach you for the last hour." She sounded more than a little upset.

"I told you, I am in an important meeting," He let out a sigh of exasperation. His wife was the love of his life, but she could be one irritating bitch when she wanted to.

"Well, I wouldn't have kept calling if it wasn't important. You need to come home right now!"

"I told you I am…"

"I know… in an important meeting." She sounded fed up and they had only just started talking. He could almost see her eyes roll. "Well, this is far more important than anything you could possibly have to deal with. Your daughter was almost raped this evening."

Benny immediately looked toward Sully.

"The little bastard." Benny decided then and there he would take care of the kid himself. His free hand slipped into his pocket and caressed the brass knuckles. He wanted to enjoy the kid's begging, his pleading.

And his bleeding.

"Did you hear what I said?" Harriet asked. "Your daughter needs you."

"I heard," he mumbled back. "I'll be there shortly."

"Benjamin?" she asked. "Is Sully with you?"

"What?" Benny pulled his mind back from his thoughts of death and destruction.

"Is Sully with you?" his wife repeated. "Clara wants to see him. I think it might calm her. She said if it hadn't been for him she'd be dead in that alley. He rushed in and saved her."

"What?" Benny shook his head. What was she saying? Sully didn't attack her? He saved Clara?

"Clara said he was like a knight in shining armor. He came out of nowhere. She said she didn't know he was so strong. She said he almost killed the guy before the bastard ran away."

"Papa, is Sully with you?" Clara sobbed into his ear, "I have to see him. He walked me home, but then he hurried off."

The Greek wracked his brain. When did Max tell him he saw Clara and Sully together? Wasn't it just before they left? What was originally planned as a dinner meeting to give the kid a raise had instantly become a last supper for the kid.

Now this...

"Papa, is Sully with you?" his daughter asked again.

"Yes," Benny said with a sigh. "He's here. I'll be home soon, baby. I'll bring him too."

He hung up his phone and walked over to Table 6. "Change of plans. Max, bring the car around the front," he ordered. "The kid's coming home with me. Drop us off and take the rest of the night off."

Max set his fork down and left for the car. Duncan moved to stand by the door.

Benny walked towards table seven and waved at the waitress. "Check."

He always paid in spite of his arrangement with Henry. The staff deserved their tips after all, and The Greek tipped 50%.

Benny picked up his coat and hat. "We need to leave," Benny said. "Clara needs you."

Sully's eyes widened as he set his fork down and pulled the napkin from his lap. "Is she okay?"

Now The Greek noticed Sully's bruised knuckles. He must have had on his leather gloves when he took the guy on. It had been a cold day and an even colder evening.

"Why didn't you tell me?" Benny asked.

"Clara thought it best if she told you. We knew you didn't approve of me seeing Clara, but I just had to see her today. I just ran into the situation. I'm sorry I damaged your faith in me Mr. Castellanos, but I am not sorry I was there for Clara." He stood and grabbed his coat. If he was lucky, he'd be out of a job and would have to walk home.

If he wasn't lucky…

He swallowed hard.

The waitress came up and placed the bill on the table. "I can take that for you," she offered.

Benny reached into his coat pocket, pulled out his wallet and laid four one-hundred-dollar bills on the table. "Keep the change."

"Oh sir, that is way too much," Cindy protested. He hadn't even looked at the bill.

"This night has turned out better than I had planned. You were a part of that. Take this as a token of my appreciation," Benny replied. He put his arm around Sully's shoulders and walked him to the door. "Clara's waiting. Let's go, son."

The Loaner

Brian K. Larson

Ellie looked over Jack's shoulder at the reservation list, "It's a good thing Mr. Claymore is running late. Table Seven's last party hasn't left yet."

Jack looked over his shoulder at the smiling woman, "Don't think for one minute that you won't have a full load tonight. Remember? Cindy's new. You'll need to shadow her to make sure..."

"... She stays in line, Jack?"

"Exactly, Ellie. At least we're on the same page... and wipe that foolish grin off your face!" Jack pointed.

"Why, whatever are you talking about, Jack?" Ellie coyly asked.

"Nothing, nothing at all," Jack glanced back at the smiling woman.

"Give Mr. Claymore another ten minutes due to the weather out there, okay?"

"Sure thing, Jack," Ellie nodded before glancing over to the new waitress. "Speaking of keeping the newbie inline, I better go check on her now."

"That's a great idea, glad you're finally doing something constructive."

The door tinkled as it opened inward. A man stepped inside, stomping the fresh snow from his shoes. He brushed the flakes from his shoulders and held his leather satchel tightly as he looked around the restaurant. Removing his felt fedora, he glanced over to the podium a few feet away.

Ellie leaned over to Jack's ear, "Sorry, looks like this might be my reservation. You check on Cindy while I attend to his lonely-looking man."

Jack pointed another stern finger in her face, "You behave yourself, Ms. Evergreen."

"Oh, now don't you worry, Jack. I'll be a perfect lady."

"Yeah, uh huh, sure you will."

The man watched the woman sway her hips as she stepped over to the man, "You must be Mr. Claymore."

"Y-yes, thank you... um, I'm s-so sorry. I'm s-several minutes late. My cab got stuck on the ice a few blocks back."

"You must be freezing, poor dear," Ellie smiled and began to reach for his tightly gripped briefcase, "Here, let me take that for you..."

Before she could touch it, Mr. Claymore yanked his hand away, "No! I'll keep it with me, thank you... s-sorry, I-I've just had... oh, never mind, you don't want to be bur-burdened..."

"Nonsense, Mr. Claymore," Ellie assured, "Your table will be ready in a few minutes. How about a nice drink at the bar? Nothing warms the soul more than a good shot of the Whisky, now does it?"

"S-Sure, I could use a nice s-shot."

"Right this way," Ellie said, exaggerating her hips for the man as he followed.

Ellie led the man to the bar and patted one of the stools, "You sit right here. Jack will get you anything you want, and I'll make sure your table is nice and cozy."

"T-Thank you, M-miss."

"I'll be right back, now."

Mr. Claymore sank onto the bar stool. He placed his bag on his lap and set his wet hat on the bar just to his right.

"What'll it be, Mister?" Jack asked from behind the bar.

"I-I'm not sss-sure. The lady here s-says a s-shot of whisky to warm me up, but I don't think anything will make me wa-warm."

"I've got just the cure for that nasty outside weather we're havin'," Jack smiled at the man as he set a glass in front of him.

Taking a set of tongs, Jack clinked three chunks of ice into the glass and then reached behind him for a flask. The ice cracked and popped as he poured the gold elixir.

Mr. Claymore picked up the glass and swirled it against the light, inspecting the meager contents.

"Gee, ii-is that all there is? I don't even think this one's a full s--shot."

"It's not quantity, Mr. Claymore, its quality... it has a distinct *quality* about it. You'll see. Go ahead, try it."

Mr. Claymore lowered the glass below his eyes and looked at the man, "Oh? And wh-wa-what are the 'qualities' that make this s-special? A-And how m--much is this gonna ru-run me?"

"Relax, Sir," Jack assured before leaning forward and whispering, "This special elixir is renowned for bringing good fortune."

"Pfff," Mr. Claymore scoffed, "ye-yeah, s--sure... bring me good fortune. Not li-li-likely."

"Sorry?"

"Yeah, it's just... it's been a rough week... I-I don't wa-want to burden you with the details."

"Go ahead and drink it," Jack insisted, "If nothin' else, it'll warm you up."

Mr. Claymore raised the glass up to this nose to take in its aroma, "How much?"

"Tell ya' what, Mister," Jack smiled as he cleaned more glasses with his white towel, "This one's on the house. You can make it up to me when those riches find you. How's that sound?"

"I-I don't kn-know," the man hesitated, "I can't ta-take on any more de-debt." He set the glass on the bar and he waved his hand, "N-No thank you."

"Come on, Mister. I'm only pulling your chain. Really, it's on the house... it's the least I can do for harassing my customers."

"O-Okay," Mr. Claymore raised the glass and downed the golden liquid.

Mr. Claymore coughed, stood up, then sprayed the bar with half the liquid.

"O-Oh m--my! I-I'm s-s-s-so s-s-s-sorry!"

Mister Claymore grabbed the towel from Jack's hand to wipe up his mess. He tried to pull the glass from his hand, but it crashed and shattered into a hundred pieces on the bar. Other patrons grabbed their half empty drinks and stepped away from the man.

"You s-s-see?" Mister Claymore complained, "E-Everywhere I go d-disaster st-st-strikes!"

"Now, don't you worry about that, Mister Claymore," Jack said with raised eyebrows, "Oh look, here comes Ellie now. I think your table is ready..."

"S-Sure thing, I'm s-sorry about the glass... okay? Ju-just put it on my t-t-t-tab."

"No, Sir! It's on the house, remember?"

"Mister Claymore," Ellie said as she helped the man steady to his feet, "Are you alright?"

"Y-Yeah. I-I'll be okay."

"Right this way, Sir. Your table is ready."

"T-Thank you... I-I don't know if I should s-stay. I-I might cause more d-d-damage... I don't really want t-t-to, b-bu-but I-I can't help it s-s-sometimes."

"Hey, we all have our bad days. Don't worry about it."

She pulled out a chair and the man sat down. He scooted closer to the table and set his satchel on the floor between himself and the wall.

Ellie handed him the laminated menu and recited the night's specials, "Tonight we offer Duck confit, Lobster linguini, and my favorite is the blackened chicken breast."

"I-I think I s-should s-stay away from anything b-b-blackened... it infers that s-something got burnt."

"How about the duck?"

"Y-Yeah, I think I would like the d-du-duck. What comes with it?"

"It's comes with mashed sweet potatoes and fresh green beans sautéed in a garlic butter sauce... trust me," Ellie said, squeezing the man's arm, "it's very good!"

"I-I thought you s-said the chicken was your favorite?"

"Yes, I love the chicken too, but the duck is out of this world, if you like duck... which I don't... but you'll love it!"

"O-Okay, I'll t-try it."

"Great... anything else?"

"I'd love a c-c-cup of hot t-t-tea. Do you have Earl Grey?"

"We sure to, Mister Claymore. I'll be right back with that."

Ellie departed to give the chef the order and to prepare the tea. Mister Claymore opened his satchel and laid out on the table a folded document that appeared to be several pages in length. Then he took out a piece of paper and set it out next to the folded document. Next, he removed a set of car keys and placed them on the side of the document opposite the paper.

The new waitress, Cindy eyed the man's odd behavior. Curiosity got the best of her, and she made her way across the restaurant.

Mister Claymore gazed down, deep within his briefcase. He focused on the revolver at the bottom. He had already decided would happen tonight.

Glancing up from the case, he saw the waitress approach. He removed one last item, then closed and latched the case before Cindy arrived. He placed a single scratch-off ticket on the table with the rest of the items.

Cindy stopped at the table and introduced herself, "Hi, my name is Cindy," her green glistening eyes spoke to the man.

He gazed up into her bright eyes and couldn't help but smile.

"Hel-l-lo."

"I'm sorry, but I couldn't help noticing. I'm so sorry."

"F-For what? My s-st-stuttering?"

"I know what those papers are... I've actually seen some just like that."

"How d-d-do you know what th-th-they are?"

"They're divorce papers, right?"

"Yes, b-bu-but how did you know?"

Cindy pulled out the empty chair and sat down. She set her elbows on the table and rested her chin in her hands. She looked into his eyes, "You wanna talk about it?"

"N-No, n-n-n-not really. Y-You better not st-stick around... b-ba-bad things happen to p-p-pe-people that are around me... I c-c-ca-can't help it really."

Cindy patted his forearm, "Oh don't be silly! It'll be fine, I'm on my break now. So tell me what happened."

"O-Okay. I-If you're not g-going to get into t-t-t-trouble."

"No, it's fine, really!"

Ellie brought out the man's hot water and a bag of Earl Grey tea, "Here's your tea, Mister Claymore," turning to the new waitress, "A word, please?"

"I'm taking my break," Cindy never took her eyes from Mr. Claymore, "Besides, Jack already told me to make sure the customers are happy. And I'm just trying to give Mister Claymore, here, some Holiday Cheer, you know... make them happy..."

"Is she bothering you, Mister Claymore?"

"N-No, actually, s-sh-she's quite nice... no b-b-bother... none at all."

"Okay, Mister Claymore. Your duck will be ready in a few minutes."

"Th-Thank you," he nodded as he poured the hot water over the teabag.

As he set the hot urn on the saucer, his finger nicked the handle. The steaming water spread over the table.

Cindy jumped up as hot water drained down the edge of the table and into her lap. She grabbed one of the spare napkins and began dabbing up the mess, careful to contain the spill from getting to the papers spread out on the table.

"S-See? I b-b-br-bring b-b-ba-bad luck everywhere I go."

"Well," Cindy quickly answered, as she sat back down in the chair, "I don't believe in silly superstitions... well most of the time, anyway... so, Mister Claymore, you can tell me all about it, okay?"

"W-Well, last week my wife s-s-s-served me with those d-d-di-divorce papers," Mister Claymore pointed, "Sh-She s-says we have no m-marriage."

"How could she say that? You seem like a very nice man to me. Do you know what went wrong?"

"Sh-She says I work too much. I have b-b-b-been gone a lot. Sh-She s-said sh-sh-she's through not having me h-home."

Cindy pointed at the pink paper, "What's this one?"

"Th-That is my notice of layoff... D-d-do-doesn't that s-sound ironic?"

"You got laid off from your job? Why?"

"C-c-com-company c-c-cu-cut backs... M-My department got d-downsized."

"Well, maybe she'll take you back?"

"N-No. Sh-She already s-s-sa-said no... I-It must be b-b-be-because she found another man... I think th-th-th-that's what really ha-happened."

"You poor man," Cindy said, squeezing his arm once more, "You must feel awful!"

"And my c-c-ca-car was s-st-sto-stolen last n-night."

"Wow, Mister Claymore, you really have had a rough week!"

Ellie set the duck confit in front of the man, "Here you are, Mister Claymore. I hope you enjoy it. Is there anything else you need?"

"Y-Yes... I-I'd like a p-p-p-piece of apple p-p-p-pie after I enjoy this wonderful looking d-du-duck," Mister Claymore smiled up at Ellie.

"No problem, Mister Claymore," Ellie glanced at Cindy, "Isn't your break about over? You have other customers to wait on."

"I know, I know," Cindy shyly acknowledged, and then turned to the man, "I'm sorry, I have to get back to work." Cindy took a step, then turned back, "I have a feeling everything will turn out alright for you, Mister Claymore."

Cindy glanced at the lottery ticket, "Mister Claymore! You never even scratched that ticket yet!"

Mister Claymore nodded as he looked up at Cindy's green eyes. Taking the ticket in his hand, he stretched it out to Cindy, "H-here, you t-ta-take it... I won't b-b-b-be needing it... n-n-not after t-t-to-tonight anyway," he finished under his breath. "You've b-b-be-been so nice t-t-t-to listen... n-n-no one ever listens t-t-t-to me, s-s-s-so you can have it, okay?"

Reluctantly, Cindy took the ticket from him and stuck it in her apron, "Thank you, Mister Claymore. Thank you very much!"

Mister Claymore raised a fork full of duck as Cindy walked away.

As soon as he had finished the dinner Ellie delivered the warm apple pie, topped with a fresh scoop of homemade vanilla ice cream.

As he finished his desert, Mr. Claymore patted his stomach. He couldn't help but smile.

Ellie brought the check to the table. Mr. Claymore pulled a crisp one hundred dollar bill from his vest pocket and wrote a thank you note on the check.

Methodically he placed all the items back inside his satchel. He stood to leave, but the tablecloth stuck to his belt. The left over dishes crashed loudly to the ground.

Mr. Claymore frowned sorrowfully as he looked at the mess.

Cindy ran over from her section, "Mister Claymore, are you alright?"

"Y-Yes... I-I'm okay, b-b-bu-but I d-d-do-don't think the d-d-di-dishes are."

"Now you don't worry about a thing, Mister Claymore, I'll clean this up in no time. You try and have a pleasant evening, okay?"

"Y-Yeah, I will... at least I won't have t-t-to worry about b-be-being s-so clumsy."

Cindy paid little attention to his last words. She looked up from the floor and gave the man a smile as he grabbed his satchel and walked out of the restaurant into the cold, bitter night.

Cindy swept up the broken dishes. Suddenly she remembered the lottery ticket.

She pulled it out and placed it on the table. Her hands shook as she pulled a quarter from her apron.

"I really need to check this ticket!"

Cindy vigorously scratched the grey pigment from the ticket. When the numbers were revealed, she gasped.

It was a big winner.

She screamed and dashed out of the restaurant into the cold winter storm.

Shivering, she looked down the street one way and then the other. She yelled, "Mister Claymore? Mister Claymore! Where are you, Mister Claymore!?"

The sound of a gunshot echoed down the street and deep within a dark alley.

Her heart stopped as she thought of what the man had just done. She took off running in the direction of the gunshot.

At the end of a dark alley, she came to a man lying face down in the snow.

"Mister Claymore! Mister Claymore, are you alright?"

She turned the groaning man over. His eyes shot open as he grimaced. She noticed his satchel laid next to him, a single bullet hole in the side. Then she saw the blood oozing from a wound from the man's waist.

"What happened, Mister Claymore?" Cindy asked, pressing her apron on the wound.

"I was taking a short cut and slipped on the ice. The gun accidently went off and shot me!"

"Mister Claymore," Cindy asked with a stern finger pointing at the man, "You didn't try to kill yourself tonight, did you?"

"Well," Mister Claymore began, "I was going to... with everything that happened to me this week... but... that wonderful meal, and talking with you, I decided not to."

"Hey," Cindy exclaimed, "You're not stuttering anymore!"

"I'm not, heh-heh, am I!"

Cindy took the winning ticket and stuffed it into his pocket, "Here, you won big tonight, Mister Claymore. I can't take this from you... you need it more than I do!"

"I won? I won the lottery?" Mister Claymore grimaced.

"Yes... you won five million dollars, Mister Claymore!"

"I did?"

"Yes, you did! Seems as if this is your lucky night, Mister Claymore."

"I suppose your bartender was right."

"Right about what?"

"That drink he gave me... he was right about good fortune coming my way."

"You just rest here, Mister Claymore. Help will be here soon, okay?"

"Yeah, thank you for everything, what was your name?"

"Cindy."

The ambulance arrived to take the man to the hospital as Cindy kissed his forehead, "You take good care of Mister Claymore, okay?"

"Yes, ma'am, we sure will."

Cindy waved at the man as they loaded him on the stretcher. She turned and headed back to the restaurant, in hopes that her new boss would be forgiving.

When she told Jack the story, he just smiled. "Well, that's just table seven…"

Star Struck

Theresa Snyder

"You're late. You better shake-a-leg. Fred's been asking about you," Donna picked up another armful of linens. "Where have you been?"

"I had an audition and it ran over." Tony headed for the locker room behind the kitchen. He pulled out his white shirt and black jacket. "It went really well. They had me read twice."

"Well, I hope you get it." Donna smiled at the budding actor. This had to be over two-dozen auditions he'd been on since he started at Hunter's Bar & Grill over a year ago. "Until then, put a move on. You need this job to pay the bills until you get rich and famous." She winked at him and left.

By the time Tony finished dressing, the piles of table linens were already gone. The silverware settings were depleted, so he grabbed a tray and started loading it with glasses. He headed out to the restaurant floor to face the music from Fred, the Maître De, and his immediate boss.

"Mr. Anthony Alzaro, you are late!" Fred said the minute he came through the swinging doors. Full name, not good. "These tables will not set themselves."

He gave Fred his most winning smile. "But I may have gotten the part."

Fred shook his head, "Theater folks are never on time."

Fred placed his hands on his hips in for emphasis. "And that is supposed to make me happy? I will have to look for a new waiter. I hate training new hires." He smiled at Cindy, the new young waitress. This was her first day. "Unless they come previously trained, which is not usually the case."

Cindy smiled back and gave Fred a thumbs-up. She had come over from another restaurant when Fred, scoping out the competition, offered her a better paying slot at Hunter's.

Tony danced around the tables placing the glasses. "You want to hear my audition number?" he asked Fred and the other members of the staff.

Fred nodded and the others agreed. Tony had a great singing voice and was always trying out for something. Frankly, Fred wondered why he never landed a part. Maybe he just didn't have the right 'look.' He was tall, dark and thin. The kind the girls swooned over whenever he entered a room. Perhaps they couldn't find a leading lady to match his height.

Tony broke into his song, placing the glasses as if it were part of the routine. The staff picked up the pace to keep up with the rhythm. The room was set and ready for business by the time the young man finished singing.

The room burst out in applause. "I think you should sing that instead of the birthday song if we get any tonight," Donna said. Tony was the soloist for any birthday celebration at Hunter's.

"Well, I think it may have landed me a place in the chorus at least." Tony tucked the empty tray under his arm and headed for the kitchen.

The first few guests were seated shortly after the 4:00 opening. The staff went to work, filling water glasses, delivering mixed drinks, and taking dinner orders.

The new gal Cindy was doing fine with Tables nine and ten. Tony noticed she seemed very comfortable and at home even though it was her first night with them. Of course, walking past table seven every trip didn't hurt any.

The McGregor's asked for Tony's section. They were regulars. Max owned a high-end jewelry store in the area and his wife loved showing off his product. They were an older couple, but Sophia still turned heads. Tonight she wore royal blue velvet with a diamond and sapphire necklace, earrings, bracelet, and ring to match. Enough shine to put your eyes out.

"Good evening, Max…" Tony nodded to the older gentleman, as he filled their water glasses. "You are looking lovely this evening, Sophia." He winked at her. This was a game they played and Max played along.

"Hey you… Don't be flirting with my gal," he said in mock irritation.

"I'm sorry, Sir. She is just too beautiful not to." Tony reached for her hand and brought it to his lips for a light kiss. "If you ever want to dump this guy," he nodded toward Max, "we could still run away together."

Sophia giggled like a school-girl, even though she was old enough to be his grandmother. "Oh, you are the smooth talker."

Tony released her hand and turned to Max. "The usual for you tonight?"

"Please," Max confirmed.

Tony brought them their martinis and sent their order of calamari and the petite filet mignon into Joel.

When he arrived with their steaks Max asked, "Had any auditions lately?"

"I have indeed. In fact, I tried out this morning for 'Dancing the Night Away.' They are prepping it for Off Broadway." Tony literally beamed.

"How exciting," Sophia said. She picked up her glass and saluted him. "Here is to your success!"

Max toasted him as well. "Success!"

After Tony left, Sophia lowered her voice to talk privately to her husband. "I wish he would get something. He tries so hard."

"There are a lot of talented folks who don't get noticed, Hon. That's just the way life is, I'm afraid." Max dug into his steak.

The kid was dashing enough, the type younger girls fawned over. But he was just too tall for a leading man's role in the theater. He would never make it past the chorus. If he wanted to make movies maybe they could stand his leading lady on a box, but in live theater, he just wasn't the right type.

"Remember when we came for your birthday last year? His voice was so incredible." Sophia took a sip of her water. "Maybe we should encourage him to do recordings instead of acting."

Max grinned at his wife across the table. She was always trying to manage everything and everyone around her. "Whatever you think, Hon. You can make the suggestion. I thought his voice was nice too."

When Tony brought their Crème Brule for dessert, Sophia suggested the recording idea.

"Oh, I don't think so," Tony replied. "I really like the interaction with the audience. I don't think I would like being cooped up in a studio all day. But, thank you for thinking I am good enough to make a record." He smiled and headed off with their plates.

The McGregor's left him a nice tip, as usual, and waved at him as they left, so the night started out well.

His next seating was an elderly widowed gentleman, and his younger daughter. He knew them by sight, but not by name. He knew she was his caregiver and he enjoyed quail every so often. He once told Tony about how he used to travel to hunt quail, duck and pheasant. He talked about his deceased wife on occasion. Tony didn't want to seem rude, but often had to cut him short to move on to his other guests. The daughter understood and they often exchanged knowing looks over the old man's head.

The third seating at that table lingered for over two hours. From what Tony overheard, they were writers and discussing a project they were working on together. He didn't mind that they lingered. They made up for it in the generous tip they left.

Next was a well behaved family of four with two children in their early teens. Hunter's wasn't the kind of place you brought a small child. The atmosphere was quiet and the piano music in the background soothing.

Three businessmen came in for a late cocktail and hors d'oeuvres after the family left. One man ordered a dessert and coffee before pushing on. They lingered for over an hour and a half with their spreadsheets and tablets. Tony shook his head when he saw the minuscule tip they left.

The last seating was a young couple. They must have come from a nightclub. They were a bit disheveled from dancing and a bit too loud, because they were already a bit drunk. The later guests didn't seem to pay their eruptions of giggling much attention. In fact, the place was pretty quiet by then. Tables six and seven each had businessmen in suits. Table nine had a gay couple finishing up their shared tiramisu. Table 11 was just putting their coats on when the nightclub pair motioned for their check.

Tony checked them out and Hanson, the bus boy, cleared the table. Tony had reached the end of his shift.

Pursuant to Fred's routine, they all gathered in the kitchen, split up their tips to give Hanson a portion and then they would go their separate ways. However, Fred had something else in store for him tonight.

He called him to one side. "Tony, when do you think you might hear about the part you auditioned for today?"

"Honestly I'm not sure. The director said he and the producers were going to discuss it until they had a cast lined up. They want to start rehearsal as soon as possible. He said maybe late tonight or early in the morning. He was going to text us when they made up their mind, so they wouldn't wake us if we were asleep."

"Have you checked?" Fred asked.

Tony pulled his phone from his pocket. It was in sleep mode, but it didn't show any alerts for text messages. "Nothing yet."

"Can you stay a little longer," Fred asked. "Henry and I wanted to talk to you."

Oh boy, what was this about? Was he going to get fired? He'd been late before and they hadn't been upset. He had made it before opening. "I'm sorry, Fred. I would have called in to tell you I was going to be late, but the director had the stage manager confiscate our phones. I guess he hates being interrupted."

Fred didn't respond other than to say, "Get into your street clothes and meet us in the restaurant."

When Tony returned to the floor, Fred and Henry were sitting at table seven.

Henry waved. "Come on over."

Tony hesitated, then took a deep breath as he walked over to the table and sat down.

Donna came out of the kitchen with three coffees and one tiramisu. She set a coffee down for each of them and the tiramisu in front of Tony. When Tony gave her a questioning look, she just smiled and shrugged before she tucked the tray under her arm and headed back toward the kitchen.

"Eat up," Henry instructed.

Tony picked up his fork, but hesitated. "I get the feeling this is my last meal."

"It is," Fred said, "at least as an employee. You are welcome to come back anytime as a customer."

Tony couldn't believe it. Maybe being late today was the last straw. This had really come out of nowhere. "I'm really sorry. You know I can't promise to not do it again, but I will promise I will call."

Henry shook his head. "Eat up, Son."

"I can't lose this job. I'll do anything you say," Tony offered. "You want me to do kitchen duty as punishment, I'm in for it hands down."

Fred put sugar in his coffee, stirred and then tapped the edge of his plate with the spoon to draw attention back to his dessert. "Kitchen duty is out of the question. However, you are required to eat your tiramisu."

Any other time, he would have been delighted with the house special, it was his favorite. But tonight, with this news, he could hardly stomach it. He stuck a fork in the cake and took a mouthful. Before he had a chance to swallow, his phone buzzed.

"I am so sorry," he apologized. He reached in his pocket to check the text. In the split moment before he read it he thought it was probably the director telling him he didn't get the spot in the chorus. It would be just his luck. No job, and no part. However, when he looked it was from the director. He wanted him to call if he was still up even though it was after midnight.

"Do you need to take that?" Henry asked.

"Ah… It's the director for the show I auditioned for this morning. He wants me to call." Tony kept staring at the screen. Why would he want him to call? Maybe they were going to have call-backs, and he made the first cut.

"If he texted you this late, it must be important," Fred said. "So call him already."

Tony looked up into Fred and Henry's smiling faces.

"Call him, Tony," Henry urged.

Tony got up from the table and walked a few steps away before dialing. "This is Anthony Alzaro. You texted me to call you."

Fred and Henry listened to Tony's end of the conversation with knowing looks on their faces.

"Sure…" Tony said. "Of course… I can be there tomorrow." He turned back toward Fred and Henry. "It just so happens that I am free… Yes, eight o'clock sharp." He hung up. "I didn't get the place in the chorus," Tony beamed at Henry and Fred. "I got the lead!"

Tony did a little happy dance in the middle of the restaurant floor.

Donna, Ellie and Cindy rushed out from the kitchen door. Ellie threw her arms around him, "Ya did it Love!"

"I did! I did!"

"I knew you could do it!" Donna chimed.

"Congratulations!" Cindy added.

"Good job Tony!" Jack and Joel patted his back.

Fred and Henry looked at each other, raised their coffee cups and clinked them together. "I love happy endings," Fred said.

Soft Heart, Open Hand

Brian K. Larson

Foster paced outside Hunter's Bar and Grill in the cold. Snow had begun to fall again in the early hours of the morning.

Nervously, Foster lowered the ski mask to cover his face before heading for the front door. Pulling out his revolver, he cocked the hammer back on his empty gun, ready to move forward with his plan. He just hoped his accomplice had done their part and left the front door unlocked.

He slowly reached for the handle, then drew his hand back, paused, and reached out once more. He pulled his hand back again and paced in front of the door.

"Dang!" Foster quietly said to himself. This is harder than I thought. I don't know how Iggy does this over and over... I'm a nervous wreck..."

Foster reached for the handle once more, bound to go through with it in spite of his reservations. With Iggy's coaching, it should go just fine. He needed to do this job. What else was there for him? Desperate times meant desperate measures.

He managed to touch the handle with his gloved hand, and held his empty weapon at the ready as he tried the door.

Locked...

"Damn!" Foster cursed, "Now what do I do?"

He looked through the small curtained windows on the door to see who was inside before darting from the view as he saw someone glancing his way.

"Crap! I think they saw me!"

Foster hid the revolver inside his jacket as footsteps approached the door.

The lock clicked before the door creaked open. An older woman poked her head outside, peering at the shivering man.

"May I 'elp you, Ducky?" Ellie tilted her head. "Come in, love, or ya'll freeze to death!"

The man nodded and stepped inside. The nice woman closed and locked the door behind him, "It's pretty late," Ellie nodded, "What're you doin' out there? It's our closin' time"

"I-I was, just, I was hoping for a piece of... piece of pie... yeah, and a hot cup of coffee too, yeah, that's it."

Foster looked around the room at the workers clearing tables, putting chairs up, and cleaning floors. Dishes clanked in the kitchen. Foster panicked. He couldn't go through with it.

"Of course, love," Ellie cheerfully said, "Ow 'bout taken' off that hat? I think I've got the perfect table for ya'.

Ellie motioned for the young man as she led him to table seven.

Foster removed his ski cap and shoved it in his pocket on top of the gun, "Foster," he nervously said, "name's Foster Bishop, Ma'am. Thank you. I'm pretty hungry," he let slip.

Ellie pulled out the chair for Foster and smiled. "I'll be back in a jiffy, Love!"

Foster continued to fidget in the seat as he looked for his inside accomplice.

Cindy carried a pot of coffee to Foster's table and filled his cup.

"Didn't you get my text?" Cindy whispered.

"No," Foster returned with a whisper, "They turned off my phone earlier..."

"I said it's a 'no go'! Do you understand? You *can't* do this..."

"But," Foster said. Holding the hot cup with both hands, he blew on it, "I am pretty committed, Cindy. I have no choice," his voice increased in volume.

"You don't understand, Foster," Cindy again whispered, "You don't have to do this at all. Don't you see? This is Table Seven."

"What's that have to do with anything?"

Foster was interrupted by Ellie, who brought him a slice of apple pie alamode and set it in front of him, "What 're you two goin' on o'bout?"

"I-It's nothing, Ellie," Cindy nervously answered.

"I'm so sorry, Mister Bishop, Cindy is new and needs to learn not to be a pest with customers..."

"Cindy's not being a bother," Foster's hand slipped into his pocket.

Ellie interrupted Foster once more, "Cindy, I think this gentl'mon would like to enjoy his pie with'ot being bother'd."

Foster pulled his hand from his jacket. The gun crashed loudly to the floor.

Ellie gasped.

Cindy shrieked.

"Oh NO!" Foster yelped as he reached down for his weapon.

Fred and Jack ran towards the commotion, but froze when Foster stood and pointed the revolver at them.

"Hold it right there!" Foster nervously pointed the gun, "This is a stick-up!"

Cindy stood by Foster and rested a gentle hand on his shoulder, "You don't need to do this," she whispered to his ear, "I tried to tell you not to do this!" Cindy finished raising her voice.

Jack held his hands in the air with Fred, "You're in on this, aren't you, Cindy?"

Fred stood next to Jack, "I figured something was wrong about our new help!"

Cindy quickly answered, "It was Iggy's idea that I get the job at Hunters. I unbolt the front door when we're closing, and Foster comes in and we take what we can and run... but that was before I saw that there was something about Table Seven."

"Put the gun down, Son," Jack instructed. "Cindy's right about this particular table. Something always, how shall I say, *unique*, happens to anyone seated here."

"I'm afraid I can't stop now. I'm sorry... Cindy, you need to stand with the others..."

Cindy reluctantly stepped away from Foster and stood by Ellie. Tears welled up under her eyes before she looked at Foster, "No, baby, don't do this. There's still time to change your mind."

"It's already too late for me, Cindy."

Fred held his hands in the air as he examined the gun. "I'd listen to your girlfriend, son. She's right. You've already sat at Table Seven..."

"... nothing's happened to me, yet, so I don't believe you!"

"Yes it 'as," Ellie reported, "Cindy didn't go through with it... in fact, she was tryin' to tell you just h'ow. Love, it's already 'appened."

"I've seen a good doctor nearly give up, but sitting at this table reminded him of his worth. I've witnessed the reuniting of a father and daughter after years of being separated. A woman who thought she was being dumped, instead became engaged and then there's the guy who lost everything! His wife, job, everything gone, Foster. He was going to kill himself tonight, but then discovered he had a winning lottery ticket. This table sparked a new hope in everyone who sits here."

"Don't forget about Tony getting the big part in the production tonight. He sat here too," Fred nodded.

"Yeah," Jack agreed, "and that leaves me short a body too. Son, if you put down that gun, I won't call the cops. Don't worry, make the right decision, and you can start working here. Come and work for Hunter's tomorrow night."

"Really?' Foster said, lowering the gun slightly, "You would? You would hire me?"

"Yes, son, I think you have great potential. Just put down the empty gun, and everything will be alright. Will you do that, son?"

"Well..." Foster slowly grew a smile, "I've never been given a chance like this..."

"This is your first robbery, isn't it, son?" Jack said, pointing at the lowering weapon.

"Y-yes... I'm scared to death about going to jail... Iggy, told me it would be an easy score..."

"It's time you started to think for yourself, Foster," Jack said, "Don't listen to those so called friends anymore. Listen to your family... listen to us."

"You would consider me part of your family?"

"I told you there was something about Table Seven," Cindy smiled. "All you have to do is put it down."

Foster carefully held the weapon in both hands. He examined the gun and glanced back and forth to Jack before he gently set it on table seven.

Cindy cried and ran to Foster. She wrapped her arms around the young man and placed her head on his chest, "You made the right choice, Foster. You made the right choice."

Ellie chuckled before she slid the pie to Foster, "Here, you still need t' eat this, because it' ain't gonna be wasted... now eat up, Love."

Jack smiled as he watched Foster take a large piece of pie, smothered in the ice cream, and shoved it into his mouth.

"That's just another night at Table Seven."

All Good Things…

James W. McAllister

"Did you shut the lights off in the kitchen, Joel?" Donna stopped with the key in the door.

"Yes, Donna. And the oven, and the burners too. I left the walk-in on, though."

"Ha-ha, funnyman. Good night, Joel," Donna turned the key and pulled it out of the lock. She grabbed the handle and gave the door a tug.

"All set?"

Donna patted the stained wood, running her hand over the varnished surface.

"All set, Fred. A good night, wasn't it?"

"Same as always, gorgeous. Up for a nightcap?"

"You buyin'?"

"Well, just this once… again!"

"Funny!" Donna slid her arm into Fred's and rested her head on his shoulder.

"Ellie had a good night. Did you see her smile when she left?"

"Table Seven does that to you," Donna smiled and squeezed Fred's arm. "The city is so pretty at this time of night, don't you think?"

Fred sighed as he took in the twinkling skyline.

"Who are you giving to tomorrow?" Donna asked.

"I thought Cindy. I think she understands, given what happened tonight."

"You're so sweet," Donna sighed. "It doesn't seem cold at all, does it?"

Their footsteps crunched into the night…

About The Authors

Theresa Snyder writes science fiction, fantasy, paranormal and personal experience stories and novels. You may find more of her writing on her website;

www.TheresaSnyderAuthor.com

https://www.facebook.com/booksbytheresasnyder/

Brian K. Larson writes science fiction, fantasy, and paranormal stories and novels. You may find more of his writing on Amazon at

https://www.facebook.com/SecretOfTheCrystal/

https://www.amazon.com/s/ref=nav_signin?ie=UTF8&field-keywords=Brian+K.+Larson&search-alias=&

James W. McAllister writes science fiction, fantasy, and paranormal stories and novels. You may find more of his writing on Amazon at;

www.amazon.com/James-McAllister/e/B00DA1ZSFI/

https://www.facebook.com/FortiterPublishing

www.ingramcontent.com/pod-product-compliance
Lightning Source LLC
Chambersburg PA
CBHW020644130626
46552CB00003B/1399